Molly *and the* Magic Dress

William Norwich
illustrated by M. Scott Miller

A Doubleday Book for Young Readers

For Joan and Ned, your family and friends,
and most especially Gorg—thank you for
the holiday memories.

W. N.

C.E.J. and Fever—for your love and support.
I am truly thankful.

M.S.M.

A Doubleday Book for Young Readers
Published by Random House Children's Books
a division of Random House, Inc.
1540 Broadway
New York, New York 10036
Doubleday and the anchor with dolphin colophon are registered trademarks of Random House, Inc.
Text copyright © 2002 by William Norwich
Illustrations copyright © 2002 by M. Scott Miller

Visit us on the Web! www.randomhouse.com/kids
Educators and librarians, for a variety of teaching tools, visit us at www.randomhouse.com/teachers

Library of Congress Cataloging-in-Publication Data
Norwich, William.
Molly and the magic dress / by William Norwich ; illustrated by M. Scott Miller.
p. cm.
Summary: Molly lives with her mother in a fancy Manhattan apartment, where she is lonely
except for her cat and her magical dress that turns her into anyone she wants to be.
ISBN 0-385-32745-5 (trade) 0-385-90844-X (lib. bdg.)
[1. Clothing and dress–Fiction. 2. New York (N.Y.)] I. Miller, M. Scott, ill. II. Title.
PZ7.N828 Mo 2001
[E]–dc21
00-040509

The text of this book is set in 15-point Bodoni Classic Roman.
Book design by Liney Li
Manufactured in the United States of America
January 2002
10 9 8 7 6 5 4 3 2 1

At first, Molly thought it was a bomb.

Slim Enid, Molly's skinny, double-jointed calico cat, dived under the covers.

"There should be a law against alarm clocks," Molly muttered. She silenced the alarm. The digital date glowed. "Not Saturday again," Molly sighed.

Saturday had always been her favorite day, a day when she and her two best friends, Bee and Jessica, got together for play dates. But this year both Bee's and Jessica's parents had taken weekend houses in the country outside New York City. Molly sometimes visited, but she always missed her mother, and Eunice, the housekeeper, and Slim Enid. (Molly's father lived in Los Angeles, and she didn't have any brothers or sisters.)

Molly pushed the covers away and tumbled out of bed. In the bottom drawer of her bureau, she found her favorite dress. It was old and torn. This was Molly's magic dress! It turned Molly into anyone she wished. All she needed to say was: "Perfect dress in a perfect world, take me into another whirl."

This morning, when Molly said, "Perfect dress in a perfect world, take me into another whirl," she became a scientist. Slim Enid was her assistant. Molly invented an extraordinary silver contraption. It made pizza, popcorn, and ice cream at the touch of one button, and when she pressed another button, it also did homework, broadcast movies, offered the coolest video games, and wrote thank-you notes for any occasion.

Slim Enid poked Molly with her tail and let her know she was hungry. "Let's get something to eat," Molly said.

Until recently, the apartment where Molly lived had resembled a palace. There had been lots of red velvet, paisley rugs, chairs and tables with carved-wood lions' paws, and ancient paintings of funny-looking people in ornate frames. But a few months ago, Molly's mother had wanted a New Look. Now everything was white—so white that Molly hadn't been able to tell the outdoors from the indoors when it snowed last week.

In the kitchen, the housekeeper helped Molly get milk out of the refrigerator. Molly was pouring some into Slim Enid's bowl when the kitchen door swung open. "Eunice," Molly's mother said, "please press this lovely new dress. Molly is wearing it to Cousin Lydia's wedding today." She looked at Molly. "No matter what excuse Molly makes," she added, "do not let her wear that ghastly rag dress of hers."

Molly's mother liked clothes, especially new clothes, and clothes liked her right back.

"Your grandmother sent you this lovely velvet dress all the way from Paris." Molly's mother smiled. "Paris, France, darling."

Molly stared at the dress as if it were a beast with big teeth.

Back in Molly's bedroom, Slim Enid perched on the windowsill and yawned. Molly dug her hands inside the pockets of her magic dress.

"Perfect dress in a perfect world, take me into another whirl," she whispered.

Moments later, Molly stood on a platform. She was running for mayor.

"When I am elected, you can wear what you want, and there will be no more Saturdays without play dates!" she declared.

The people, and Slim Enid, cheered.

Molly's bedroom door opened. Instantly Molly turned back into her real self. Eunice entered.

"What's the matter, dearie?" Eunice asked. "Most little girls would love to dress up and go to a big fancy wedding."

"I'm too short for weddings." Molly sighed. "I can't see unless I stand on the pew, and no one will let me."

"Maybe there will be some cousins your age to play with," Eunice suggested.

"There weren't any last time. Cousins don't come out of thin air, you know."

Eunice and Molly made Molly's bed. Slim Enid dived underneath. "I remember when I was young, I often felt like you do today," Eunice said. "Sometimes I felt strange even in the middle of friends and family. You know what that feeling was?"

"No," Molly answered.

"I was homesick."

"Homesick? How could you be homesick if you were home?" Molly asked.

"That's why it was so strange," Eunice said. "I felt homesick, but homesick for something missing inside myself."

Molly tried to look inside herself for what was missing. It made her feel woefully dizzy.

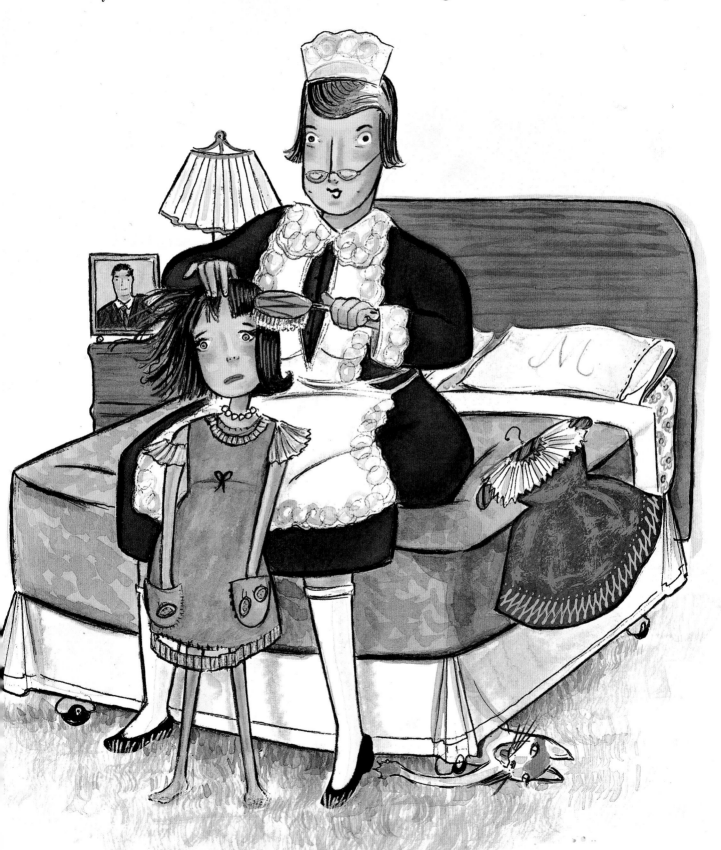

When Eunice left, Molly put the new dress on. It felt stiff.

She took it off and put on her magic dress. "Perfect dress in a perfect world, take me—"

"Molly, take that dress off, and hurry up. I am waiting," her mother announced over the apartment's intercom system.

How did she know?

Molly put the new dress on again. She made a face as if she'd just kissed a thousand lemons, and curtsied in front of the mirror.

"I hope you've fed the cat properly," Molly's mother called over the intercom.

A meow came from under the bed.

Molly rushed. She stuffed her magic dress into her book bag, grabbed Slim Enid, and plunked the cat inside the book bag too.

"I think you'll like wedding cake," Molly told Slim Enid.

"You look lovely, Molly," her mother said, helping Molly with her coat.

"I look like a stuffed bird," Molly said.

"Oh, what a good idea to bring your book bag. But if you want to read, well, I suppose you know to wait at least until dessert is served."

Molly wasn't paying attention. She was thinking about Slim Enid. For a skinny cat, Slim Enid certainly was heavy. And Molly hoped the cat would keep still.

"Uncle Todd is downstairs," Molly's mother said.

Uncle Todd wasn't really Molly's uncle. He was the young gentleman who had helped Molly's mother redecorate the apartment.

"New dress, Molly?" asked Gus, Molly's favorite elevator man.

"Isn't it marvelous, Gus?" Molly's mother said.

"Pretty as Christmas," Gus said with a smile. "And so is Molly."

The car taking them to the wedding was driven by a chauffeur. "How do you do," Molly said to him. "I'm Molly. What's your name?"

"I'm Joseph, miss."

"We'd rather be going to the movies, Joseph," Molly said.

"Molly, stop that," her mother scolded.

Uncle Todd smelled like grapefruit. Molly's mother smelled like gardenias. "You both smell," Molly said.

"Thank you," they answered.

The church was filled with merry people and music.

"Darling, love your hat," Molly's mother told the woman seated next to them.

"Typical," Molly observed. "Not one kid my age."

As the wedding procession began, Molly stood up on her toes to see the bride walk down the aisle.

"Forgive me if I cry, Molly, but weddings always make me tear up," Uncle Todd whispered as he edged Molly toward the aisle.

Molly didn't feel at all tearful. She was too busy looking at Cousin Lydia's dress, which had a train at least a hundred feet long.

After the ceremony, a newspaper photographer took Molly's picture. "Hello, child," he said, smiling. "What a pretty coat and dress!"

Then Uncle Todd, Molly's mother, and Molly got into the car. "To the reception, please, Joseph," Molly's mother told the driver. "At the Knickerbilt Club."

Fifth Avenue was bumper-to-bumper traffic.

"Lydia seemed so happy," Uncle Todd said.

"Yes, happy at last," Molly's mother responded.

The car crawled down Fifth Avenue. Through the windows, Molly watched the people walking by. Everyone seemed to be doing, and wearing, exactly what they wanted.

When the car stopped at a red light, Molly noticed a woman on the sidewalk. She was all alone. Her tweed coat was in shreds. Her gray hair was matted. The woman poked through a trash can for food. Molly felt very sad.

"There but for the grace of God go we," said Molly's mother.

The traffic light turned green. The car inched away.

The Knickerbilt Club was very grand. It had a brick facade, high ceilings, and fireplaces in every room.

The waiters looked like penguins. Molly asked for a root beer.

"Not at the Knickerbilt," Molly's mother said.

A waiter brought Molly a glass of ginger ale.

The wedding guests greeted each other with great cheer. They kissed on both cheeks, but missed mostly and ended up kissing the air.

Molly tried it.

The air did not kiss back.

Molly settled herself in a large chair and opened her book bag. Slim Enid's head shot up like a balloon. Molly gently patted the calico cat back into the bag. "Just wait a little bit, please, E.," she said. "Till no one is looking."

"Molly, you can read later," her mother said, suddenly at her side. "Mingle, darling, mingle."

Molly was almost clobbered by dancing people and their happy knees.

A while later, Molly's mother and Uncle Todd deposited Molly at her table.

"We're nearby, darling," Molly's mother said.

Molly sat between two great-aunts, Aunt Sheila and Aunt Deeda. Across the table were her two teenage cousins, Patrick and Paul.

The two great-aunts spoke in a grand way, as if they had mashed potatoes stuck to the roofs of their mouths. They were discussing a woman named Bunny, who seemed to have gone to a flower show in London and caught a flu. Bunny was quite an unusual name, Molly thought, for someone who wasn't actually a rabbit.

Meanwhile, cousins Patrick and Paul went on and on about someone named Muffin. Muffin this and Muffin that.

Sometimes it was very difficult to understand her relations.

Time for an escape. Molly asked a waiter for a glass of milk. As soon as he brought it, she left the dining room. She climbed the stairs to the next floor of the club, where she discovered a large, handsome room filled with books. No one was there.

Molly unzipped her book bag. Slim Enid's head popped up.

Molly took out her magic dress, then set the glass of milk down for Slim Enid. Quickly Molly slipped the magic dress over her head and over her new dress. She had barely said, "Perfect dress in a perfect world . . ." when she became a beautiful bride climbing a huge wedding cake.

Molly scaled the cake's mountainous sides of slippery vanilla frosting. It was hard work. With her bouquet, she fought off the wild beasts hiding under the flower decorations.

The sound of a door handle turning startled her.

"Molly!" her mother exclaimed. "Take that dress off right now!"

Uh-oh, Molly thought. *Caught in the act.* Well, not really. But just getting caught wearing the dress was trouble enough.

Molly didn't argue or try to explain. She simply apologized.

"I think the trick with aunts like Sheila and Deeda is to try to imagine them as little girls," Molly's mother said. "Believe it or not, they were once your age, and I promise you, there were days when they felt just as you do now."

"Where have you been, dear?" Aunt Sheila asked when Molly returned to the table.

"Climbing Mount Wedding Cake," answered Molly.

"Climbing Mount Wedding Cake?" Aunt Deeda smiled. "We've all been up that hill, dear."

Dinner was served. "Fish eggs? Mega-yuck," Molly said when a slice of caviar pie was placed in front of her. But Slim Enid couldn't have been more pleased. Molly slipped the pie inside the book bag, and the cat ate every morsel.

After three more courses, cousins Patrick and Paul were still talking about Muffin, and Aunt Deeda, for some reason, was whispering to Aunt Sheila in French. With no dessert in sight, Molly felt the urge to make another getaway.

This time, rather than going up, Molly went down through a door that said BASEMENT.

Better put on my magic dress, she decided, upon reaching the lower level. As she did, Slim Enid escaped through the open doorway.

"Slim Enid?" Molly called after her. "Wait for me."

Molly entered a dim room.

"What are you doing, silly cat? This could be enemy territory," Molly warned.

The calico cat came out, and Molly stroked her fur.

Looking around, Molly noticed a tattered tweed coat on a chair. Then the door of what she assumed was a closet opened. Fog and steam poured out. In the mist appeared a woman wrapped in white towels.

Molly screamed! The woman screamed!

Slim Enid scurried under the bed.

"Who are you?" the woman asked as the mist cleared.

"Who are *you*?" Molly responded.

"Johnny, the weekend doorman at the Knickerbilt, lets me use this empty room to freshen up," the woman explained. "Says I bring him good luck. Don't know about that. Johnny would be fired if anyone found out. Please don't tell a soul you saw me here."

"I won't," promised Molly as Slim Enid crawled out. "If you promise not to tell a soul you found *us* here." Molly scooped up her cat.

The woman nodded and smiled.

Molly smiled back. "Where do you live?" she asked.

The woman gestured toward the ceiling.

"I don't understand," said Molly.

"On the streets," the woman explained.

Molly recognized the coat over the chair. It belonged to the homeless woman they had seen during the car ride to the wedding reception.

The woman picked up her coat. Underneath was her old dress. "I should be on my way," she said.

Slim Enid's paw tugged at Molly's magic dress. When Molly didn't respond, Slim Enid tugged again.

"Oh, what a brilliant idea!" Molly exclaimed. "Please, ma'am, don't put on your old dress. Put *this* dress on," she said, taking off her magic dress.

"I can't do that, miss. It's yours."

Molly insisted.

"But it won't fit."

"Yes, it will," Molly promised. "It's a magic dress. You'll see. Think of what you want to be, and pull it on over your head as far as you can. Then make a wish."

The woman hesitated.

This didn't stop Molly. "I say a spell that goes like this: 'Perfect dress in a perfect world, take me into another whirl,' but you really don't have to say it for the dress to work. Just act as if you believe."

The woman sighed.

"Please try the dress on," Molly pleaded.

The woman slipped the dress over her head as far as she could.

"You can become a princess," Molly said.

"I'm too old to be a princess," the woman answered.

"Then how about a lawyer?" Molly said. "Or a doctor. Or a scientist."

"Or the Queen of England." The woman laughed.

They heard footsteps in the hall.

"Hurry," Molly said.

Everything happened very quickly then. First Molly's mother burst into the room; then came Uncle Todd and Johnny, the Knickerbilt's doorman, followed by cousins Patrick and Paul. Even great-aunts Sheila and Deeda! No one looked pleased.

"We're toast!" Molly said.

But rather than screaming and yelling, there was silence. Mouths dropped. Molly saw why.

They were all staring at the Queen of England!

The magic dress had worked better than ever. Molly was thrilled.

"Oh, dear," said the queen, just as the real monarch might. "Look at me!"

Everyone remained frozen with surprise.

"Well," the woman said confidently, "I'm late for an important date."

She opened her handbag. There was nothing inside. "Have you a hundred-dollar bill, perchance, that I might hold for you?" the queen asked Uncle Todd.

Uncle Todd took a crisp bill from his wallet and bowed.

The queen smiled and waved, then proceeded to make her way out of the room.

Aunts Sheila and Deeda curtsied as she passed them.

Only Johnny, the Knickerbilt doorman, recognized the woman. And he was so happy he cried.

They all followed the queen upstairs. The bride curtsied. The groom bowed to the floor.

The waiters brought the queen a slice of caviar pie.

"Tasty," she said. "Needs a root beer."

"But we don't have root beer at the Knickerbilt, Your Majesty," the waiters apologized.

"We are not amused," the queen said. "That will not do." She took Molly's hand.

The guests followed the queen to Fifth Avenue. Slim Enid rode in Molly's book bag with the zipper wide open. Near the Hotel Pierre they saw Eunice getting out of a taxi.

"I've been frantic, looking for Slim Enid all afternoon," Eunice cried, joining the procession.

A hot dog vendor gave the queen and Molly free root beers. Another vendor insisted they accept free ice cream cones. The newspaper photographer took the queen's picture. She slept in one of the city's best hotels that night.

After the story about the queen appeared in the next day's newspaper, she got a job advertising chocolates. "Long live the crunch" is the line she made famous.

"I think you were very wrong to run off like that," Molly's mother told Molly when they got home after Cousin Lydia's wedding.

Molly said she was sorry.

They lit a fire in the fireplace in the all-white living room.

"You could have been hurt, Molly," her mother said. "I'm so glad you weren't. I love you very much. And I learned a lot about you today. I'm sorry you feel lonely so often." Molly's mother looked around the room. "I think we need some of our old things back, don't you?"

Molly smiled.

"And maybe a new magic dress?" suggested her mother.

Molly shook her head. "I don't think so. One magic dress was amazing enough."

Now Molly, her mother, Eunice, Uncle Todd, and the woman who became queen have tea-and-root-beer parties every Saturday afternoon at the Knickerbilt Club.

Slim Enid, too. She is crazy for that caviar pie.

JE
NOR

DATE DUE

4/16/02	3/25	
2/17	MAY 1 4 2007	DEC 0 9 2016
May 5	OCT 1 2 2007	
1/8	SEP 1 0 2008	
5/19	AUG 2 1 2009	
6/15	10/5/9	
8/04	FEB 0 5 2010	
9/2	JUL 0 8 2011	
8/05	SEP 1 6 2011	
	MAR 2 2012	
AUG 9 2005		
	MAY 0 9 2012	
8/1/05	JUL 3 0 2014	
APR 0 7 2007	NOV 1 2 2016	
FEB 2 1 2009	MAR 2 5 2019	
AUG 0 7 2015	MAY 2 2 2019	
GAYLORD		PRINTED IN U.S.A.
	SEP 0 4 2020	